POND
WATER
RIPTIDE

...

BRENDA FIREEAGLE BIDDIX
RIAN MILETI

Written by: Brenda (FireEagle) Biddix, Rian Mileti

AUTHORS

Brenda F. Biddix was born into the stark, natural beauty of an Appalachian hunting cabin in November 1950, marking the beginning of a life journey characterized by resilience, creativity, and profound change. With a degree from the Newspaper Institute of America, Brenda refined her craft in creative writing and expanded her expertise into psychiatric and clinical nursing, drawing deep insights into human resilience and the spirit. Despite a significant, life-altering accident in 1991, Brenda emerged as a relentless advocate within her church and community, fervently mentoring youth and combatting domestic violence. She poured her resilience into crafting Inside The Pain: A Survivor's Guide to breaking the cycles of abuse and domestic violence.

Her literary contributions have not gone unnoticed, earning her an Editor's Choice Award and a nomination for Poet of the Year in 2004 by the International Symposium of Poets. Brenda's eloquent words have been featured in *Lamplighter Magazine, Cherokee Sentinel, 'The Colors of Life,'* and *'Labyrinth of the Mind: A Poet's Muse.'* Facing Parkinson's Disease as a side-effect of arsenic poisoning presented a new challenge, but her spirit and creativity found new life. Thirteen years later, her desire to write was still alive even though Parkinson's became a huge barrier. Through doodles and descriptions, she developed the concept for *'Pond Water,'* and this thrilling sequel, *'Pond Water Riptide.'*

Rian Mileti, a devoted father and fierce friend, is the accomplished author of seven books, including the acclaimed *'The Color Gone.'* Known for his narrative prowess and humble demeanor, Rian prefers to let his storytelling capture the hearts and minds of his readers. He got his skills from his grandmother and best friend, Brenda.

Their collaborative efforts on *'Pond Water'* not only met but exceeded expectations, achieving #1 best-seller status on Amazon across multiple categories. *'Pond Water Riptide'* is not just a sequel but a continuation of their mission, carrying its hidden messages within its pages. The sales from these books directly support Brenda and others with Parkinson's by covering medical expenses and home modifications not covered by insurance. This initiative is a testament to their shared journey.

Thank you for being part of this meaningful journey. Your support makes a significant difference in the lives of those affected by Parkinson's Disease.

Below are some of her original sketches, which add depth to our shared experience. To avoid spoilers and enrich your understanding, a section titled **'The Silent Story'** has been added to the end of this book.

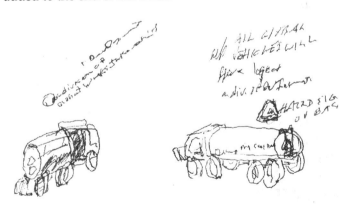

ADVENTURE AWAITS

NEXT

SCAN ME

BOOK

THRILLER

SCI-FI

VISIT
RianMileti.com

Contents

HUNTING IN THE NIGHT

THE NIGHT WAS ALIVE with gunfire, echoing through the woods. They jumped in the truck when they realized where she was heading. Jared's breath fogged up the windshield. It swirled like the turmoil churning inside him. The ringing in his ears was a relentless reminder of the chaos that had just unfolded.

Jared's hands, visibly shaking, struggled to retrieve a pill bottle from his pocket. The sound of pills rattling against the plastic seemed unnaturally loud. Taking one, Jared let out a heavy sigh, "You see this?" he coughed, gesturing to the bottle. "The poison… it's pulling me apart. I think these tremors are getting worse."

"I hope you don't lose it like she did," John voiced.

The image of the woman, Bobbie Jo, haunted their minds. After being discovered alongside a body, she managed to escape into the forest. The toxic waters of the local pond had changed her. She wasn't just a strange neighbor anymore.

As Jared revved the engine, it gave life to their silent promise as military men—that the bonds formed on the battlefield were unbreakable. Bobbie Jo was racing towards their friend Allen's home. Once more they had found themselves at war. They were determined to get there before she did.

Jared's truck tore a furious path through the countryside. His tires screeched in protest, challenging the worn, winding roads as he drove. The scene of flickering police lights vanished behind them. Now, they were alone in their race against the unknown, on a mission to protect their friend at his home.

Shadows of trees passed overhead, casting skeletal patterns across their path. An ominous silence enveloped them, reminiscent of the foreboding calm before a storm. Jared's grip on the steering wheel tightened, his knuckles turning white. He was not going to let her harm Allen. She had already killed someone and vandalized his house. He had had enough.

There it was, Allen's secluded cottage, shrouded in a silence too profound, too unnerving. Had they arrived too late? Jared and John leapt from the truck.

Their steps were swift and deliberate as they raced to the front door.

"Allen!" Jared's voice echoed through the stillness. "Allen!"

They searched every room, every corner, but there was no sign of him. Jared's frustration grew with every unanswered cry, the silence taunting their urgency.

"Jared!" John shouted, "He's out here!"

Jared's hurried footsteps echoed as he reached the back porch. Allen was found frozen in a rocking chair, staring out at the creeping tide of shadows.

The moon revealed his pallid face, each breath drawn in shallow gasps. Kneeling, Jared noticed that Allen was as white as a ghost. But this wasn't what bothered him, it was his expression. His eyes sunken into his skull, the life being torn from his soul. His expression was a testament to the cost of memories too heavy to share. Allen still needed crutches to get around. He was a sitting duck. Allen had been listening to the gunshots whispering through the woods. But Jared needed to tell Allen what was happening, to explain that the deranged woman was closing in.

Jared tried to rouse him. "I know you can barely walk buddy, but we have got to get you inside. Something is..."

With a low moan, Allen pointed a shaky finger toward the looming trees signaling that she was already here.

Their eyes locked onto the approaching woman. She tore through the shadows with unsettling speed. She was frantically clawing at the ground, crawling toward them. She moved fast even though her limp legs dangled lifelessly behind her. Danger hung in the air, thickening with every heartbeat...

THERE YOU ARE

THE WOMAN CRAWLED through the darkening field. Jared's heart raced as her form came into focus. A grotesque figure, dragging itself across the ground. The encroaching clouds made her movements almost otherworldly. Storm clouds rolled in as she pulled herself closer to them. The bite of the cool breeze wasn't just felt on Jared's skin—it seemed to invade every fiber of his being. The swirling mass of the night's events congealing in his mind.

Jared's fingers clenched around his phone. An instinct to protect Allen surged through him. As he turned to face her, a sound cut through the field like a thunderclap. Gunfire caused the woman's body to jerk along the ground; an unearthly howl escaped her lips.

They emerged from the shadows. Police officers, clad in dark uniforms, approached with cautious but firm strides. Their guns still trained on Bobbie Jo. The harsh glow of their flashlights revealed their stern faces. They were stressed beneath layers of dirt and sweat.

The lead officer, with a no-nonsense demeanor, stepped forward. "Shots fired! Suspect down!" he announced on his radio, his voice booming across the field. His tone suggested she'd attacked an officer in the woods. Turning to Jared and his companions, "Everyone alright over there?"

Jared, still processing the surreal turn of events, managed to nod. "Oh yeah, just gotta help our friend here inside. Were any of the officers hurt?"

The officer spared him a brief glance before turning his attention back to the woman on the ground. "She attacked two of us in the woods. You all should consider yourselves lucky we got here when we did."

John and Jared supported him under each arm. They lifted Allen from the chair on the porch and helped him into his home. They were mindful of his recent injuries.

Allen sat wrapped in a blanket, his gaze distant, lost in a storm of shock and disbelief. Jared's concern for him was evident as he gently asked, "You okay, man? I haven't seen you like this before." His voice was sincere as he looked at Allen, who seemed lost within himself. He knew that look because they both had been on a battlefield together.

Stillness overcame the room. It was a stark contrast to the distant, muffled chatter of officers outside. It was eerily fading into silence. Allen's gaze was fixed on the open window. Through it, the curtains danced like phantoms in the evening breeze. They were the only witnesses to the night's harrowing events. His lips parted, a silent plea for words that refused to come. His eyes were endless pools of torment, strangled by a million unspoken words.

The room's air grew heavy, charged with an unspoken dread that Jared felt clinging to his skin like a cold sweat. He noticed the subtle disarray. Allen had abandoned his chair, its angle suggested a hasty departure. A faint impression still marked its cushion. What had caused Allen to go outside? Jared's eyes followed Allen's gaze to the window and out to the field beyond. He pictured Allen on his crutches, watching something near the trees moving. Outside, the field lay bathed in moonlight. The deep shadows seemed to be lengthening as if reaching for something inside the house.

Jared, heart pounding, knelt beside Allen, whose fear was a tangible presence in the dimly lit room. "The tree line?" he ventured, his voice barely a whisper, tracing the line of Allen's sight. Allen's response was a sudden, sharp focus, a silent scream in his eyes. Jared's throat tightened. "You saw something before the gunfire, didn't you? What was it, Allen?"

Allen's pupils shot towards the door, his body tensing. A low moan escaped him, as if he were trapped in a nightmare with no escape. Jared pressed, "Did you see someone else?"

Their eyes locked, a silent understanding passing between them. Allen had seen someone else, someone still alive, lurking in the shadows outside. His eyes showed that they were still coming for him. An eerie silence filled the room as the officers outside went quiet. There seemed to be something moving around the house. The porch outside creaked as something approached the door.

WHO'S THERE?

AS JARED OPENED the door, a sudden tightness gripped his chest. It was not from the crisp night wind, but from the unsettling sight before him. In the distance was Bobbie Jo, being wrapped in plastic. Her hand was visibly missing fingers, twisted. Jared's breath hitched. He realized she had been attacked. An officer stepped forward, silhouetted by the deep glow of the porch lights.

"Jared, I wanted to personally thank you again for today," the officer spoke at the door. Jared listened but found it hard to focus. "Did she harm anyone in there? We noticed your friend limping when you helped him inside."

Jared shook his head, trying to ground himself. His mind was alive with unanswered questions. After taking a breath, he recalled, "Allen was recently discharged from the hospital and is still recovering."

"Thanks," the officer replied, nodding toward Jared. "If you hadn't tipped us off months ago, who knows how many more people she would have attacked. The town thanks you." The officer concluded, "Get some rest. If you need anything, just let us know."

Closing the door, Jared turned to Allen, "What did you see?"

Allen hung his head, silent.

Jared looked toward the ceiling, "This isn't over, is it?"

Allen's muffled agreement was chilling.

John quipped, "Nothing like a bit of doom and gloom to lift our spirits, eh?"

"She was running from something," Jared revealed, his voice tense with emotion. "Her hand looked like it had been in something's mouth. I thought she had gotten back at that man who broke into her place, but I'm not sure what Allen saw."

A buzz from John's phone captured everyone's attention. Pulling it from his pocket, he read some updates from the EPA. "Jared, it looks like there's another dumpsite," John explained. "I believe the company that started the toxic waste dumping just moved their operation. They're over in Salvo now. I need your help, Jared."

"What do you need me to do?"

"Why not head down to where this report came in? You know my place in Salvo. The cabin down by the ocean, you're welcome to take it over. Maybe you can figure out what's really going on? Bring a stop to this before more people are pulled into it. I'm only there maybe twice a year. And I'm asking you because, you're the only one I trust right now. After seeing what we saw today, this needs to be stopped right now. Seeing how bad Bobbie Jo got from this, I can't imagine. If we can catch someone in the act, or some company, we may be able to bring an end to all this."

Waving goodnight to Allen, Jared invited John out to his truck. The police had vanished, leaving the night eerily quiet. The night air, heavy with the scent of impending rain, whispered secrets only the darkness knew. The clouds rolled in, and the moonless sky silenced even the rustling leaves. The night's events had etched a permanent scar on Jared's psyche, his imagination taunted him. He was on edge to the point he felt the trees were talking.

As John settled into the passenger seat, he could see Jared's face. "Can you give me a ride back to the pond? We're draining it tomorrow. Whatever secrets it holds are going to come out."

As they drove off, the road led them back to the still body of water, its surface reflecting nothing but the darkness around them. The engine hummed a low dirge as they paused, looking out at the water. A black sheet of glass amidst the trees. It's poison drove Bobbie Jo into madness and almost claimed Jared as well.

John's truck was waiting on them, but Jared couldn't shake this feeling of doom. The water, with its murky depths held secrets he didn't know. The pond was a grim reminder that some doors, once opened, could never be closed again. Whatever poisoned the water, was still out there.

Something echoed from the water as John swung open his door and stepped out onto the grass.

JARED'S MISSION

REACHING INTO HIS pocket, John handed him the key to his cottage in Salvo. "If you get lost, just give me a call."

"What do you need from me?" Jared insisted.

"Eyes, ears, and boots on the ground. I'm going to head back to Allen's place. I'm going to try and get some sleep before we drain this thing."

The pond was still but it was so dark outside, he could only see what his headlights illuminated. Jared noticed the large tanker truck next to the pond. It was ready to remove the rest of the toxic water at first light. John was heading the whole operation to clean up the site once and for all.

Jared nodded, his voice strained as he replied, "Godspeed, John. Be in touch, my friend. I'll let you know when I get to the cabin."

Jared waved goodbye, as John shut the door. He watched as John got in his vehicle and its engine rumbled to life. The sound of their brotherhood was still alive. As he pulled away, Jared's red taillights glowed in the darkness, a beacon of departure. The rearview mirror offered one last glimpse of the pond that started it all. He could only imagine what awaited in Salvo.

A few hours passed as his imagination came to life. What was in the pond to cause Bobbie Jo to do that? A feeling came over Jared, a slight tremor that caused him to swerve back into the road. Would he recover from being poisoned? He took a deep breath and watched the rain fall through his headlights for the rest of his journey. It was time to plan. Drawing from past experiences Jared knew he was limited to what he could do. Gathering local paperwork and advice would be a start. He knew his phone was about all he had to gather evidence with, besides his truck.

Jared found himself stepping off at a gas station, a couple hundred miles away from Elmhurst. The rain had stopped but the night wasn't over. A newspaper dispenser outside the gas station featured a large headline. As soon as his eyes fell on the words 'Vandalism in Elmhurst,' he turned his gaze away. It seemed the news was starting to spread. It was only a matter of time before the reporters got ahold of him.

"I need to stay away from the spotlight for a while," Jared muttered to himself. His voice was a mix of frustration and fear. "I'm almost at John's place."

With the moon pushing through the clouds, he decided to call Allen to let him know he had arrived. John was probably asleep by now, but Allen didn't look like he was going to sleep tonight. Maybe an update call would bring Allen some relief. Sitting there at the gas station Jared looked around as the phone rang. He wondered if Allen would even say anything.

The phone picked up, and Jared heard breathing.

Jared sighed, relief filling his chest. "Hey buddy, I'm glad you answered the phone. I made it out here to the coast. The news of my house being vandalized by Bobbie Jo has made its way out here already. I just saw it on the local newspaper."

Allen listened… strained breathing was all Jared could hear.

"I'm still trying to process everything as well," Jared concluded. "I wanted to call and make sure you're safe. Anyway, I hope things haven't gotten that bad out here yet."

Jared could only make out the sound of Allen getting comfortable. A cup being set on a table, not much else.

"I'll keep you updated Allen. Did you get any sleep last night?"

Allen's heavy breathing turned into a sigh.

"You got this, buddy. Remember, we're in this together, and I'm only a few hours away. If you need to vent, I'm here. Alright?" he assured, before hanging up the call.

Jared stepped into the gas station, the air thick with an unsettling quiet. Thinking back, not a single car had pulled in while he was on the phone. The place was barren and chilling. The usual buzz of activity was absent. The door was propped open by a mere rock. It seemed oddly out of place. Wait, why was the door like this? There wasn't even a clerk to greet him from behind the counter. Instead, only the gaping maw of emptiness stared back. Questions clawed at his mind, piercing the silence: What was going on in this town? Had the poison already started to spread?

AMONG THE LIVING

JARED'S EYES NARROWED as he heard a voice call out to him, "Ahhh, I've been wanting to talk to you…" their voice etched a strange tone in the air.

A man stepped from behind the isle. The strange man with a sinister grin approached Jared with his hands behind his back. Tension filled the air. The man was middle-aged with a touch of gray in his hair. "You're in a hurry," he smirked. "I've seen a lot of people with the same expression over night. You went to that county fair, didn't you?!"

"No," Jared responded tersely. "I'm out here working."

"Really? This is my hometown! What brings you here."

"Ah, just some boring old environmental stuff.

What happened at the fair?"

The man chuckled, lightening the mood. He then went around the counter, he was the clerk. "Oh, you won't believe it. The animals in the petting zoo broke free and caused quite a mess out of the fair. Rumor is they were drinking out of the river over the few days the fair was in town. I believe, the water turned them."

"The river?"

"Yeah, you won't believe this, but you should have been here years ago. There's a factory that dumps stuff in the water. Cheaper for them, I guess. They used to be called Olympique Global Precision, but now it's Global Works."

Jared was intrigued. Did this guy solve the case already? Extending cash to him he paid before exiting the store. Jared figured it was a good idea to text John with the info. That way he could also keep track of what he learned. John quickly responded:

What do you know about Global Works?

Not much yet. Still looking into it.

Keep me updated.

I got this from a man at a gas station, so take it with a grain of salt

Putting his phone in his pocket, Jared remembered something. Did the clerk say he recognized him? After the gas stopped pumping, Jared turned to see the clerk outside smoking.

"Did you say you wanted to talk to me?"

"Oh yeah! I read all the newspapers. You were on the front this passed week, weren't you?"

"Nobody mentioned it."

"Jared, right?"

Nodding subtly he let the man continue.

"Someone wrote an article about how you were helping a veteran while he was in the hospital."

"Really?" Jared returned. "Yeah, my friend was in a car accident not long ago."

The clerk offered a conversation, "How is Allen doing?"

"In a bit of shock," Jared confessed.

"I heard that the man Allen hit was carrying chemicals that leaked everywhere. I bet it was an employee of Global Works. I didn't know if you saw anything else."

Jared paused, thinking back to how furious the man was acting. He could see his face in his mind but didn't know any of the other side. Infact, he was so consumed with taking care of Allen he didn't notice much about the man. Jared's senses were alerted, people that give out too much free information are usually not to be trusted. Without wanting to be judgmental, he chose to end the conversation here. "I'm not sure. Have a good night," Jared added opening the door to his truck.

"One more thing!" The man quipped, "If you want to investigate that company, try the docks."

Jared thanked him, nodding his head in appreciation. Sitting the door to his truck, he made his way to the cabin only a few minutes away. John's cabin was nestled among the sea oats and pampas grass that whispered with the ocean breeze. The board and batten siding of the cabin was weathered by salt and storms. It was well built, a resilient shelter against the elements. As Jared approached, the crunch of gravel underfoot broke the symphony of the coastal wind.

Stepping onto the wooden porch, he paused, taking in the scene. The ocean, a vibrant tapestry of blues and greens, stretched beyond, its surface shimmering under the stars. The air, tinged with the salty tang of the sea collided with the shore. Pampas grass, tall and proud, swayed gently, its feathery plumes created a soft halo around the cabin. Sea oats, their delicate seed heads bobbing, painted a picture of wild beauty, undomesticated and free.

Unlocking the door, he could hear the swamp echo with sounds behind him. Inside, the warm lights illuminated the rustic interior. The wooden floors, worn smooth by years of footsteps, echoed with a welcoming note as Jared moved through the space.

After a shower, the refreshing cascade of water washed away the grime and sweat, leaving a sense of renewal. Jared wrapped himself in a thick, soft towel, the fabric enveloping him in warmth. He made his way to the bedroom looking to get some rest after a long night of traveling. Settling into bed, he was ready for some sleep. He didn't know what to expect to find in this small town, but the home was quiet. As he lay there listening to the swamp, he heard the crickets slowly stop. Even the frogs faded away, all that was left was the sound of the ocean waves. It was strange. Then the rattling of a lock got his attention. The front door swung open as he sat up in bed.

"Hey! Who's there?" Jared announced as he got out of bed.

Rushing down the hall he heard someone in the kitchen. Clanking pans, the opening and closing of cabinets caused him to slow his pace. Who was in the kitchen? Peaking around the corner he could see a trail of water across the floor. Did they crawl out of the swamp? It couldn't be. Then he saw her, as she turned her piercing eyes clung to him. Bobbie Jo's hand, missing fingers clutched a pan.

"You drained my pond, MY POND!" She scoffed. "I used to collect eggs from it! So what do I use for baking, NOW?! Bananas, pumpkin, or applesauce? No, I need something with protein!" Bobbie Jo stepped forward tightening her grip on the pan. "Something with a similar nutritional profile! I want my pancakes to be fluffy in the morning."

A blank expression crossed his face…

She screeched, "I need blood!"

DINNER TIME!

LIFTING THE PAN, Bobbie Jo's snarl was chilling. "You're going to make the most beautiful pancakes!"

In a panicked reflex, Jared reached up, grappling with the pan as it swung down. The world spun as they crashed to the ground. With a sharp breath, the harsh reality of his bedroom snapped into focus. It was just a nightmare, yet his heart raced on. Now awake, he had hit the floor with a thud, tightly gripping the lamp from the side table. Having rolled out of bed, his first day in Salvo had begun.

The coolness of the wooden floor seeped into his skin. It was a grounding force that pulled him back from the brink of panic to the stark reality of his room. He was drenched in sweat, his hands trembling. He was unsure if it was the adrenaline or a side effect of the poison. He fumbled with the jacket of his coat, retrieving his bottle of pills, and taking one. Scooping up the blanket from the floor, he meticulously made the bed. Each fold was a step toward regaining control after the chaos of his nightmare. He felt rested but unsettled by the dream. The lamp's cord had been ripped from the wall, yet the lamp appeared unharmed.

After plugging the lamp back in and stretching, he stepped outside to listen to the waves. The cabin offered a panoramic view of the ocean. Scanning the horizon, he noticed a long pier in the distance. Recalling the gas station clerk's mention of the docks, he decided to investigate. Climbing in his truck, he set off through the marshlands toward the dock.

A campground with a small beach appeared. It was populated by a handful of locals who seemed to be enduring more than enjoying their time. Their faces bore the marks of fatigue. Their bodies were cloaked in an aura of nausea and weakness. They sought solace in the gentle lap of water at their feet. The sun was just beginning to climb above the horizon, casting the first light of day across the beach.

A boat cruised past, its wake creating a mist that carried on the breeze. Jared observed the smiles on people's faces. The cool mist was a fleeting respite. It momentarily distracted them. The sunrise bathed everything in a soft, golden light. Jared caught a troubling sight out of the corner of his eye. A jogger was staggering, then collapsed onto the soft sand. Concerned, Jared ran over to him, asking if everything was alright. The jogger replied, "Yeah, I just went for my morning swim and was heading back to my vehicle."

Jared's voice was firm, edged with concern, "I know what's wrong with you. This is serious. We need to get you to the hospital, right now."

The jogger laughed off Jared's concern, "Just hungry, man. Didn't get much sleep last night. I'll be alright." With a swift motion, he helped the jogger up, who sprinted off, calling back, "Thanks, though."

Jared sat back there on the beach. His gaze swept over those around him, each seeking solace in the sun's embrace. His own battle with the unseen poison trembled within him. It was a silent testament to the danger lurking unseen, driving him to save others. His tremors were getting worse. In his pocket, the pill bottle rattled subtly, its sound telling his story. This wasn't just a container of medicine; it was his mission. The quiet rattle spoke volumes whispering to him of the battle he had not yet won. It resonated with the truth of his journey amidst the blissful ignorance of those surrounding him.

Jared observed the fog, created by the mist kicked up by passing boats. Its calm cloud rolling across the ground. Could it be poisoned? He watched their laughter bubble up from the relaxing scene. They were drowned out by their music and dancing. In his mind, he imagined their pleas for help, regretting not being warned. The seed of paranoia taking root. Yet, he knew that if he spoke up now, they might dismiss him, roll their eyes, or even curse him away. He needed evidence. A reason for them to hear what he had to say.

Blinking away the thoughts, Jared questioned if he was reading too much into things. He also needed more than a hunch for himself. Right now, he was just paranoid from his dream, right?

Leaving the beach, Jared wandered to a local fishing supply store. The vibrant scene was bustling with activity. The walls, adorned with colorful lures and fishing gear, were complemented by the scent of fresh bait hanging in the air. Jared immersed himself in selecting his gear. The anticipation of a different kind of adventure took over.

The vivid scene continued as Jared cast his line into the water, near John's cabin. The rhythmic sound of the reel unwinding fills the air. The sun painted the sky with warm hues. He patiently waited, taking his mind off his problems and was simply present by the water.

The cast yielded only a small fish, which he promptly placed in his cooler. Casting out the line again, he waited. Peaking into the cooler again he noticed a bump on its head. Holding the fish in his hands, Jared felt the weight of realization settle in. The poison was not just a distant threat; it was present in the water he now held before him. Jared held the gasping fish. Its deformity glared under the morning sun. He felt a mix of vindication and horror. This was the undeniable evidence he needed. It was weaving through Elmhurst's poisoned waters, flowing into the ocean.

Plopping the fish into his cooler the ocean called to him. It had something else on the line.

THE DEPTHS BELOW

CLOUDS OF DAWN covered him as the ocean whispered secrets only the brave dared to listen to. Jared stood at the water's edge, his line cast into the gray expanse where the sea met the sky. As he felt the first tug, his pulse quickened, anticipation tightening his grip on the rod. There was a weight there, a presence in the depths was staring back at him from beneath the waves. Its shadow danced in the water.

The air around him thickened, charged with the raw essence of the wild sea. He could taste the salt on his lips, feel the mist clinging to his skin. The line strained, singing with the tension of his unseen adversary. It was a battle of wills between man and the mysteries of the deep.

Suddenly, as Jared glimpsed an abyss beneath his catch, the shadow surged and the sea around him seemed to hold its breath. Time suspended as the shadow twisted, turning back towards the depths. A fleeting connection lost as the line snapped, leaving only the echo of the ocean's secrets vibrating through the rod. The shadow vanished, leaving no trace but the swirling waters. The sea had spoken, its message as clear as his broken line... he was onto something.

With the cooler beside him, Jared felt a surge of urgency to learn about his catch. After a quick drive he stepped out onto the beach he was at earlier. He was met with the curious gaze of the locals.

"You're not thinking of fishing off the dock, are you?" a local inquired, an eyebrow raised in mild amusement. His tone was friendly yet carried an undertone of communal norms.

"Actually, I just found something," Jared insisted. "I was battling with something immense, not your average catch."

"Really?" They laughed, "How big was it?"

"Take a look at this," Jared announced, opening the cooler to reveal the small fish. A murmur of laughter rippled through the locals. Focusing on the fish's unusual features, "Look closer at its head, these aren't ordinary markings. They're mutations, possibly from pollutants," Jared explained. He hoped to spark concern and not dismissive laughter.

"You know, 4-leaf clovers are mutations, right?" One local noted, "It's the sea, is probably a scar. It's natural; it's just a fish. Get your conspiracy stuff outta here. The ocean is cleaner than the water you use for the shower, you city slicker. I've been here my whole life, it's fine." They brushed off Jared's genuine concern as he watched them turn away.

Undeterred, he loads the fish into the jeep. Jared considered his next steps. He chose the local aquarium as his destination. It was a place where experts on marine life could offer answers. Where could he find a marine biologist to talk about his unusual find?

Pulling into the aquarium he tossed his jacket over the cooler and made his way inside. His eyes looked ahead as he paid for a ticket. They warned him of the aquarium closing soon but he insisted he wouldn't be long. After a few minutes he spotted someone at the large tank, feeding the fish, he told them of his discovery. Pulling out his phone he showed them a photo of the fish. As they saw it the person made an urgent call for Dr. Simonds. Their reaction suggested this was something they'd heard about before, but this was the first time they'd had one on property. "A guest has one of the fish on site," The person panicked over the phone, "Follow me."

Hurriedly exiting the aquarium, the staffer led Jared outside. His apprehension gave way to curiosity as Dr. Simonds approached. Her keen gaze, not just on him but on what he carried, hinted at a shared concern for marine life. Jared caught a spark of something more in her eyes. It was an intensity that mirrored his own concern.

Dr. Simonds leaned in, her interest evident in the fading daylight. "May I examine the fish more closely?" she asked, her voice carrying a blend of professionalism and genuine curiosity. Her proximity and the faint scent of the sea in her hair momentarily distracted Jared. It told him that his journey was no longer a solitary one.

Jared turned and led them to his truck. As he opened the door he hesitated, his confidence wavered slightly in her presence. "I'd prefer to keep it in sight, but I need your expertise."

Jared pulled his jacket from the cooler. The container tumbled out of the car, bursting open. The fish flopped free, jerking across the parking lot.

CHASING ECHOES

IN A FLURRY of movement, Jared returned the fish to the cooler, its body limp and motionless. Dr. Simonds, urgency threading through her usually calm demeanor, beckoned him. "Hurry inside," she insisted. They rushed across the parking lot and into the aquarium. The sound of their footsteps echoing off the corridor walls. The lab was a stark contrast to the vibrant life housed in the aquarium, its cleanliness and order a silent promise of discovery. She directed him to quickly pour the unmoving fish into a tank. As the water enveloped its body, it twitched, its gills fluttering weakly against the clear, filtered liquid.

"What do you think?" Jared whispered. His voice mixed concern and fascination. He watched the fish regain its strength. Its body slowly undulated, swimming around as if testing its new home.

Dr. Simonds studied the fish intently, her expertise guiding her analysis. "It's a sea bass, but this... formation on its head is unlike anything I've encountered. It's not a tumor; it's something else. I'm not sure what it is," she mused, her brows knitting together in concentration. The room filled with a shared sense of urgency as she clicked around on her computer, hunting for answers. The hum of the aquarium's filtration system a steady backdrop to their racing thoughts. "If pollution is the culprit, we need to find out," Dr. Simonds declared, her determination mirroring Jared's own.

They stood side by side, peering into the tank, a silent pact forming between them. This mission was about more than just collecting samples; it was about bringing an end to this. Not just for the fish but to keep it from hurting other people in the community.

With practiced hands, Dr. Simonds prepared to examine the fish closer. She gently swabbed the anomaly. The fish, sensing the intrusion, squirmed away, but not before she transferred the sample to a glass slide. It was here that Dr. Simonds began to share the story that had led her to this very lab.

"When I was a little girl, my parents took me to the ocean," Dr. Simonds began. Her voice was tinged with nostalgia as she peered into the microscope. "I remember the vastness of the water stretching out before me, the way the waves danced under the sunlight. Even to this day I remember it. But it wasn't just the beauty that captured me; it was the mystery. The ocean was this huge, unexplored world filled with life that we knew so little about."

She adjusted the focus on the microscope, her eyes intent on the slide. "I became obsessed with marine life, devouring books and documentaries, anything I could get my hands on. By the time I was in high school, I knew I wanted to be a marine biologist. I wanted to explore those depths, to discover the secrets hidden beneath the waves."

Dr. Simonds paused, her gaze meeting Jared's. "But it wasn't just about exploring the unknown. Even back then, I could see how human actions were affecting the ocean. Pollution, overfishing – it all threatened the very world I was so enchanted by. I realized that understanding marine life wasn't enough; I needed to protect it too."

Turning back to the microscope, Dr. Simonds' voice grew passionate. "That's why I'm here, Jared. This," she gestured to the lab around them, "isn't just a job for me. It's a calling. Every species we can save, every bit of pollution we can stop, helps us all. Seeing this sea bass, in this condition, is heartbreaking. We have to bring an end to this for the ocean, Jared. What if that's someone's food? If we don't stop this, who will?"

Jared listened, moved by the depth of Dr. Simonds' passion. And in that moment, he knew that their mission was about more than just exposing those behind this.

Looking into records, it appeared as if the fish's mutation was a direct result of exposure to chemicals, to known carcinogens. Jared considered the other creatures in the sea and how this would effect them. How the fish got exposed to carcinogens was the new question.

Jared thought it would be best to update John on his findings. Pulling out his phone he typed,

I caught a contaminated fish this morning, decided to have it checked out. We have it back here in the lab here at the Salvo aquarium.

What did the fish look like? Can you send me a photo?

Sent

Jared took a photo of the fish in the tank, its image now immortalized as evidence of their shared endeavor. Then he brought up his concern to Dr. Simonds. "I don't really feel comfortable leaving the fish here because I need it for evidence."

"Evidence?" Dr. Simonds echoed, intrigued. "What kind of evidence?"

"I'm trying to get a company shutdown that's behind some toxic waste dumping in public areas. This fish is part of my research. If I lose the fish, the company could keep operating."

Dr. Simonds paused, her gaze shifting from Jared to the fish and back again, as if seeing both in a new light. "Could you let me watch over the fish for tonight, let me get it back in good health? I'll document everything."

"Absolutely, but my phone doesn't have your number in it." Jared smirked, sealing their unexpected alliance.

"Would love to see where you caught the fish. Is tomorrow good for you?" Dr. Simonds suggested. "I don't work weekends." As she added her number into his phone.

"Sure, I'll text you the address."

"I'll bring the fish with me. I may even take it home tonight. I want to get to the bottom of this as much as you do."

As they parted ways, Jared's journey back to the cabin was a long one, his thoughts swirling like the waters around the mutated sea bass. What other secrets did the pond hold?

Jared's phone lit up with a message from Dr. Simonds. "See you tomorrow."

"Goodnight," he sent back before turning off the lamp.

As he drifted to sleep, the snapped line from earlier that day came to mind. What could they end up catching? Tomorrow might just be the day they hook into something big…

GLOBAL WORKS

DR. SIMONDS approached Jared. Curiosity painted her features alongside a hint of urgency. She had made it. The cooler in her hand was a testament to their shared mission. It held a fish, evidence of their environmental crusade, carefully preserved inside.

"Jared, I wanted to thank you for trusting me with your fish. This specimen... it's like nothing I've ever seen. I'd only seen this kind of thing in reports, never up close—until yesterday." Handing over the cooler, she shared a bit of unsettling news, "I got a call this morning. Leaving the aquarium last night, we set off the silent alarm."

Setting the cooler on the porch of the cabin, Jared replied, "Everything alright?"

"Yeah, I just got a call and had to clear it up. When we stayed over late to tend to a fish, I got distracted. It sounds like I set off the side door alarm when I left last night. The police surrounded the aquarium. It's all cleared up now though, what are you using for bait?" Dr. Simonds shifted the topic, her professional curiosity peeking through.

"Corn," Jared revealed, a playful pride in his voice, as he displayed the can.

"Corn? Really? I brought worms," Dr. Simonds countered, a smile crossing her face.

As they cast their lines into the sea, the simple act of fishing became a backdrop to a deeper conversation. Jared scanned the horizon for more than just the day's catch. Turning to Dr. Simonds, he presented a pressing question. "Considering the challenges we're facing, how do you think we could collaborate, using your expertise in marine biology?"

Dr. Simonds' gaze lingered on the ocean, a testament to countless hours spent studying its mysteries. "The ocean holds answers to many of our questions," she mused, tying her scientific knowledge to their shared dilemma. "It's about understanding its signals and responding appropriately. Our collaboration could bridge that gap between observation and action."

As the dawn spread its gold across the sky, Jared and Dr. Simonds settled by the shore. Their fishing lines were cast into the whispering waves. The morning was serene. Fishing was peaceful. But they both knew their real catch lay in the secrets the ocean held.

While Dr. Simonds focused on the gentle rhythm of the sea, Jared's gaze wandered. The real catch of the day wasn't another fish. His eyes followed the shoreline, catching a large tanker truck hidden in the distance. A hose trailed from its side, disappearing into the water. Without a word, Jared's instincts kicked in. He began taking photo after photo on his phone, capturing pieces of a sinister puzzle.

Dr. Simonds noticed his alarm. "They're from Global Works, using sea water for irrigation," she tried to reassure. "They take water into their irrigation trucks to irrigate the field."

"No, they're dumping something." Jared's voice was tense, urgency driving him as he photographed the dark liquid streaming into the ocean.

"What?!" The revelation hit Dr. Simonds hard. "This is where the reports are coming in."

They watched a dark liquid consume the ocean around the cabin, and Jared snapped another photo.

Jared didn't hide the urgency in his voice in his reply, "I need you to show me those reports."

"I've got the folder with me, how about we get lunch and go over them?"

The decision was made without hesitation. They reeled in their lines, their earlier pretense of fishing abandoned. Jared took the fish inside before getting in his truck, prepared to follow Dr. Simonds. Looking over at the distant white truck again it looked as if someone was looking back at them with binoculars.

As he followed Dr. Simonds to the diner to study the documents, Jared saw a chilling sight in his rearview mirror. It was the white truck. Its occupants were hidden but clearly focused on them. They had not been discreet enough.

Inside the diner, Jared flipped through the reports. He connected the dots between the catastrophe and its symptoms.

"This looks similar to what me and Allen had happened to us," Jared realized. "If arsenic and lead did this to fish, then that explains why it's happening to us."

Pulling out his phone, he sent John a message containing the photos of the reports and of the truck dumping.

But it was Dr. Simonds' next words that cemented their fear, "This is the largest marine disaster reported."

John texts back,

Just dig up what you can and send it to me.

The diner's bell jangled abruptly, cutting through their conversation. Several men entered, their presence menacing. Jared's blood ran cold as he recognized the occupants of the truck from the shore.

Turning to Dr. Simonds, his voice low, he warned, "We were followed."

NO LONGER SAFE

THE DINER'S BELL dinged again. More shadowy figures entered, their boots thudding on the worn floor. Each step echoed a foreboding drumbeat in the otherwise tranquil restaurant. Dr. Simonds' eyes flickered with barely concealed anxiety. Her fingers twitched subtly toward her phone hidden beneath the table.

The fluorescent lights buzzed overhead, casting an eerie pall over the diner. Their jackets displayed a coiled serpent symbol representing Global Works.

Outside, the wind howled like a wounded animal, rattling the diner's windows. It was as if the wind was trying to warn them of the peril lurking within. Jared's face appeared calm, but his heart raced.

"Plan?" Jared whispered. The word barely escaped his lips. The clinking of silverware and the low murmur of other patrons drowned out his voice. They were blissfully unaware of the tightening noose.

"We're not leaving through the front," Dr. Simonds murmured back, her gaze darting around the room, mapping their escape with a strategic eye. "I have someone coming. Follow my lead."

A couple of the men passed by and claimed the table behind them. Two men sat at the bar near the front door watching over the exit. Jared watched as another man slowly approached their table. His boots echoed around but the brim of his hat hid his face.

Dr. Simonds moments ago had sent a simple text: "Need your help. Diner off 5th. Bring the van around back."

Smoothly she stood up from the table, grabbing Jared's hand. She led him around the bar. The server could see it on Dr. Simonds' face, something was wrong. Joining in, the waitress subtly guided them through the kitchen, past the puzzled looks of the kitchen staff.

The van's arrival was almost cinematic, cutting through the tension like a blade. It skidded to a halt in the narrow alley behind the diner. Its headlights briefly lit the graffiti-tagged dumpsters, creating monstrous shadows. As they exited the back of the diner, Dr. Simonds pulled him towards the van. She threw open the back door, urging Jared to follow her inside. The van's engine roared to life as they climbed into the back.

As they drove away, Jared's eyes were drawn to every vehicle they passed, searching for the Global Works serpent emblem. It seemed to be everywhere—on bumper stickers, hanging from rearview mirrors, like it was following them. Every glance out the back window he searched for followers. The sight of any vehicle lingering too long beside them spiked Jared's pulse. Every shadow felt like it was hiding something.

Soon, Dr. Simonds' home became a makeshift command center. The driver and another one of her friends bombarded her with questions. With a deep breath, she recounted what they had seen and their escape. A long hose draining muck into the ocean. The crew surrounded them at the diner. Her voice was steady, but her eyes betrayed the fear that lingered. After she explained what was going on, her friends made a plan. They departed, taking Dr. Simonds' and Jared's keys, to fetch their vehicles for them. It was clear they needed to stay low for a while. The other friend, Alex, stepped through the door and handed Jared his keys back, Jared's truck was safely parked outside. Alex revealed he once worked within the bowels of Global Works. "This all doesn't sound right," he mentioned gravely, "Their main mode of operation is through their delivery trucks. It's how they ship orders. They wouldn't send a shipment out to just dump it. Now, I never was a driver but that doesn't seem right." His implication hung heavily in the room; the weight of his insider knowledge lent credibility to his words. "There's got to be something else going on."

Then Jared showed him the photos and only silence followed the group. The evidence shares a different story. As everyone departed the task before them was clear, something had to be done. Jared, overwhelmed by the day's events, found refuge on the couch. Dr. Simonds offered him a blanket, their hands briefly touching, a silent thank you exchanged in the gesture. His presence was a calming force in the storm that was her life. There was something comforting about Jared.

The next morning, Jared's actions only further solidified Dr. Simonds' growing admiration for him. Despite the danger, his concern had been for her safety. He was sitting on the front porch of her house, watching over her place. She found herself marveling at his character, a rare find in the dark world they were navigating. Was it his strength? His motivation to make things better?

Dr. Simonds approached and handed him something all too familiar. A small vial for collecting samples in. He understood his mission to investigate the disposal site used by Global Works. She extended an invitation to Jared, offering her place as a sanctuary whenever he needed it. Expressing his gratitude, he climbed into his truck. He then staked out where he saw the tanker dumping and after he found it parked a good distance away. Abandoning his truck, he slipped into the woods moving like a predator, stealthily towards the suspected dump site.

The tree line offered a vantage point, with the ocean's expanse unfolding before him. He was ready, hidden amidst the leaves. An hour passed, then two; he lay there, motionless. And in the distance, he could hear it: the tanker was approaching. It passed him as a few men hopped from the front. The group ran a long hose, coiled under the tank, into the water. He pulled out his phone and began recording. He recognized all of them from the diner; he was in the hive, watching the worker bees. A black, tar-like substance filled the water, and disgust crossed his face. How could he let them just do this? Why were they doing this? It was time to find out. Reaching into his pocket, he pulled out the vial Dr. Simonds had given him. With anger in his chest, he stood up from the leaves...

IT'S TIME

THE DENSE FOLIAGE masked his presence, allowing him only glimpses of the crime unfolding before him. In his clenched fist, a vial awaited evidence. The monstrous truck finished regurgitating its bellyful of poison into the sea. The hose retracted like a serpent satisfied with its delivery. Who uses a large tanker truck to dispose so much liquid into the sea? The beach was once a ribbon of golden light embracing the ocean. The vibrant life of the coast was now suffocated under the sheen of thousands of gallons of waste.

Jared waited, the rumble of the truck's engine fading into silence. Enveloped by the pungent smell of oil and salt, he stepped into the clearing. Carefully, he scooped up the toxic muck into the vial at his fingertips, struggling to keep it steady. His tremors shook his arm as he tried to keep the muck from touching him. This shaking was evidence enough of how dangerous this substance could be.

Returning to his truck, Jared's body overflowed with frustration and adrenaline. Driving straight to Dr. Simonds' house, the vial's contents sloshing with each turn. The sample in his possession was damning evidence. His arrival was urgent, his movements frenzied as he presented the vial to her, its dark contents was a curse. Jared knew what it had already done to him. The shivering in his body was still present because of it.

"Are you alright?" Dr. Simonds' voice cut through his thoughts.

"I recognized the smell," Jared managed, the words barely a whisper. "Hey, I got it."

The transition from the muggy heat outside to the cool interior of Dr. Simonds' house was abrupt. He arrived at her door with the vial shaking in his hand. She wondered into the kitchen returning with two glasses of iced tea. The condensation beading on the glass offered a chance to settle his nerves. "I believe we can figure out what this is at the lab. But first, you look terrible," she told Jared with a mix of concern and a slight chuckle, acknowledging the day's toll on him.

Jared laughed, "Thanks, you're lovely too." Accepting her tea he pressed the cool glass against his cheek. The black vial was now sitting between them.

"You're shaking," Dr. Simonds' smile was warm, a beacon in the storm that had become their life.

"I can't stop it," Jared noted. "It slowly wears me out. It started after I was exposed to… that." Eying the vial. "It's been over a month now."

"Let's get you cleaned up," she insisted.

He smiled at her, exhaustion evident in his eyes. "Well, after I get cleaned up, do you want to head to the lab?" He noticed that lying in the woods for a few hours had given him an itchy and earthy smell. She was probably right, he needed a shower.

It wasn't long they both found themselves at Dr. Simonds' lab in the aquarium. The atmosphere was charged with anticipation. Jared tapped his fingers impatiently on the counter. Each second seemed like an eternity as he awaited the verdict of their findings. The dance of chemical reactions in the test tubes was mesmerizing. The liquid seemed to move as if it was alive. Dr. Simonds took a drop of it and placed it on a slide. Under the microscope, the truth was laid bare. The bacteria and microorganisms were mutating, their natural forms distorted by the chemicals.

Dr. Simonds stepped back from the microscope. Her soft voice filled the silence. "I did some research while you were out on Glyphosate. I was thinking about how Global Works uses it for farming and agricultural. The International Agency for Research on Cancer is getting pushback for calling it a carcinogenic, but the levels are a factor. I have a feeling it's being used more than it's supposed to be. It's been linked to birth defects, cancers, lymphoma, and tumors, like on the sea bass you found."

Jared leaned in, turning his focus on the microscope's view. The microorganisms vibrated and shifted in chaotic patterns. They seemed to be aggressively showing rage at a microscopic level. Wasting energy by thrashing around, attacking everything they touched. "It looks like these things are starving. They are eating things while being eaten. So, the chemicals are affecting everything in the water?" he pondered aloud, watching the war through the lens.

"Whatever this substance is," Dr. Simonds interjected, "it's inducing mass aggression in marine life. The sea bass was just the beginning. Microorganisms are evolving into something new, something more dangerous. I can't imagine what would happen inside someone if they were exposed to this…"

TSHHH

"Woah," Jared recoiled, his shock mirrored in Dr. Simonds' eyes. The microscope's slide had cracked, as if their discovery sought to break through into their world.

The black vial indeed tested positive for lead and arsenic. Dr. Simonds speculated, "So, I believe the traces of lead are from corrosion in the facility. But the arsenic, is an effective mosquito killer. This might be their misguided attempt to combat malaria," she mused, her voice tinged with disbelief. "There's a critical lack of understanding about how much pesticides affect the environment. Runoffs from farms and chemical dumps contribute significantly to killing life in the ocean. You can't scale up pesticide use like this; the environment needs time to heal. Coral reefs can't move and they rely on clean, nutrient-balanced water for their survival. It's frustrating when other factors are blamed and these issues are dismissed. Reefs are so fragile that they cannot recover on their own."

Jared's frustration boiled over. "So is Glyphosate present in the sample? Did I really watch them unload a tanker full of toxic waste into the ocean?" He watched her confirm his suspension, as she double checked her findings. Jared's hands trembled visibly by his sides. He didn't know if it was due to his exposure to the poison or if it was a physical manifestation of his anger. Looking at his hands he then looked at Dr. Simonds as she researched. He whispered to himself, "I can't let others go through this like I am..."

"I was talking to Alex, who worked for them, he says it's mostly state contracts," Dr. Simonds sighed. "Meaning this dumping operation is signed off by the politicians, not the people who made the chemicals. Someone obviously proved it was safe to the officials."

Before exiting the lab, he needed her to know he was doing this for more than himself. Jared reached over and hugged her, his body shaking but his heart pure. As the door closed behind him, he wasn't just going to stand by and let this continue. He might be the only one who knew what was happening. Slamming the door of his truck, he had a plan.

Hidden once more in the embrace of the woods, he waited for another tanker, ready to expose the truth. It wasn't long before another large truck pulled in. He waited until they began pouring the sludge before he stood up. Stepping out into the open, he announced his arrival, "How's it going fellas? I saw you all while I was fishing earlier." He was no longer just a bystander in the narrative of Global Works; he was now a threat to their operations.

"I haven't seen you in a while," one of the men answered Jared.

SEEING GHOSTS

UNDER THE CANOPY of a dimly lit sky, Jared found himself face-to-face with a figure from his past. The man was a ghost that had now began to haunt the edges of his memories. The beach's ambient noises faded as he stepped forward, crunching sand under his boots.

Ethan's voice was laced with nostalgia and venom as he stepped closer. "Jared, after everything we've been through, you don't remember me? I'm hurt." His words are drenched in sarcasm, a cruel smile playing on his lips, hinting at the complex history between them. His presence was barely visible against the backdrop of the dark ocean waves.

The faint smell of the sea was being replaced by the smell of chemical waste. The slopping sound of the muck draining from the truck pooled where they were standing. The starlight from tanker's shine revealed marks on Ethan's face. Marks that showed years of hardship, betrayal, and bad choices.

"Ethan Cross..." Jared murmured, the name unlocking a flood of memories. Images of a distant battlefield, the chaos of an operation gone awry, and the face of the man before him, younger, yet unmistakably the same. "What are you doing here, Ethan? I thought you were dead. Why are you involved in this?"

Ethan's laugh was short and devoid of humor. "Life took unexpected turns after you left me for dead, Jared. But that's classified, isn't it? I had to make ends meet, and Global Works offered me a way."

Ethan stepped closer, the distance between them charged with the tension of unfortunate mistakes. "But let's not dwell on old grievances. I'm offering you a chance to walk away from this. Keep quiet about what you've seen, and I can make it worth your while." Ethan leans in, voice dropping to a conspiratorial whisper. "You'd be amazed at how much we make from disposing of... unwanted elements." His eyes gleam with greed, revealing the corrupt foundation of his motivations and the moral chasm that separates him from Jared.

Around them, the night seemed to close in, the sound of the waves a distant murmur compared to the pounding of his own heart. Jared noticed, then, the subtle shift in the environment. Upon his arrival, the previously deserted beach now teemed with quiet movements. Shadows detached from the darkness, silently encircling him.

As Jared scanned the beach, he realized Ethan wasn't alone. His men emerged from the shadows, each step deliberate, closing the distance. They accompanied Ethan faceless in the night, but their intent was clear. Jared had nowhere to run. With the ocean to his back, a circle of snakes closed in on him.

Ethan's voice broke through Jared's rising panic, calm and controlled. "What do you say, Jared? Will you give me your phone?"

Jared glared at Ethan, a storm brewing in his eyes. With a shake of his head, he conveys a silent but fierce defiance. His voice steady yet charged with emotion. "I'm not for sale. You know, there's always plenty of money in the world. But I find it funny out of everything we've seen, saving the world isn't in the budget."

Ethan's men looked to him as he laughed, eyeing Jared recording them with his phone. "You really think we are going to let you out of here? With all those phone recordings?" he sneered.

RIPTIDE

A SILVER SHEEN from the moon crossed the restless waves. The ocean was now tainted with the vile secretion of illegal dumping. Ethan Cross, a silhouette against the dark horizon, gestured sharply at his men. "You've been spying on us before, haven't you?"

Adrenaline took Jared over like wildfire, but he stayed silent. Ethan's operation wasn't just illegal; it was a declaration of war, with profits soaked in poison. Jared tightened his fists as he looked around, outnumbered. It was laughable against Ethan's men, but it was all he had.

"You think you have something on us? I bet you've got some evidence in that cabin, don't you?" Ethan deduced.

Before Jared could react, a sudden strike against his head, and the world went dark.

In the dwindling twilight, Jared's vision tunneled as Ethan's shadow loomed over him, a smug grin etching across his face. Jared awoke but stayed motionless. The cold beach air, thick with anticipation and dread, became a silent witness to the confrontation that was about to unfold.

Ethan crouched down, his face inches from Jared's, the fading light casting half of his visage in darkness. "You remember me. I'm touched," Ethan's voice dripped with sarcasm, a twisted smile playing on his lips. "But memories won't save you now."

Jared's mind was alive, thinking back at how Ethan had disobeyed a direct order. He thought about how Ethan's actions resulted in the lives of many men. Ethan stared at him with detached amusement, laying in the sand. A spark of the old camaraderie they once shared flickering and dying in Ethan's eyes.

"You could've walked away, Jared," Ethan scoffed, standing up, his figure towering over him. "But you just had to play the hero, didn't you?" His mockery is sharp, a pointed reminder of their shared past. "Did you really think you could swoop in and save the day?" His question, rhetorical and biting, reveals deeper layers of their history and conflict.

Ethan turned away, signaling his men with a curt nod. Two burly figures stepped forward, seizing Jared by the arms and dragging him away any hope of escape. They moved with a purpose. Their shapes merged with the darkening sky. His legs slid across the sand toward the cabin. Jared knew the mutated fish was inside in a cooler. Right off, he couldn't think of anything else. It would be better for him to play dead until he could figure out how to escape in one piece.

Jared was thrown to the ground in front of John's cabin. Ethan approached, a can of gasoline in hand, the liquid sloshing around inside with each step.

"You know, Jared, I admired you once," Ethan began, unscrewing the cap of the canister, the harsh scent of gas cutting through the salty air. "But you've become a nuisance. And nuisances need to be dealt with."

With deliberate motions, Ethan began to douse the cabin's perimeter with gasoline. Smirking with each splash against the board and batten siding. Jared lay still, the realization of Ethan's intent settling in like a lead weight.

Ethan paused, his back to Jared, his outline was tense against the backdrop of the cabin. Ethan continued talking to Jared, even without him responding. "You don't know anything about me," he growled, the anger in his voice barely contained. "Not anymore."

Turning to face Jared, Ethan's expression was one of resolve, of decisions made and paths chosen from which there was no return. "I'm not the man you knew, Jared. That man died a long time ago."

Ethan tossed the empty gasoline can and struck a

match. The flame flickered like the last remnants of their past. He dropped the match. The flames caught eagerly, consuming the cabin. Ethan watched solemnly as the blaze grew.

The heat from the fire pressed against Jared's face, the light casting shadows that danced and twisted around Ethan's form. "It looks like he's still unconscious. Go ahead and throw him into the undertow," he instructed his men. "A fitting end to a seal, don't you think?"

As the fire grew, consuming everything Jared had fought for, Ethan's silhouette receded into the night. Ethan's men pulled his limp body into the water and as they felt the current begin to pull, they released him into the depths. Their laughter was the last thing he heard as his head dipped underwater.

CLAIMED BY THE SEA

WITH THE COLD SLAP of water against his face, Jared was floating in the ocean. His eyes flickered open, to see if the coast was clear. Before him was a nightmarish scene: the water around him teemed with mutated creatures. Their forms twisted by Ethan's chemical waste, thrashing around. The toxins in the water were clearly responsible for these horrifying mutations. All the plants and animals.

Struggling to swim in the current, the large figures twisted closer, drawn in by his movements. He needed air. The waves pulled him under, as he rolled in the undertow. With every ounce of strength he swam, but was going deeper. He was running out of time. The water was clear under the oily surface.

Someone else was being devouring alive inches away from him. He couldn't see who it was, but he knew the sea creatures weren't normal. Their gnarled teeth glinted in the moonlight. Thrashing in the rising tide, he couldn't get above the water. One creature snapped at his clothes as he swam. His lungs burned as he struggled to see. He could see things swarming all around him. One of them snapped its jaws at his sleeve, another at his pants. He ripped off one of the slimy creatures latched onto his shirt collar.

Gasping for air, he swam down the shoreline, he was finally able to breathe. Eventually he pulled himself onto the beach. Collapsing onto the sand with tattered clothes. The smoke from the cabin surrounded him, the toxic fumes seared his lungs. The realization hit him hard as he thought about his escape—Ethan had never intended for him to survive.

His clothes barely clung to him as he watched the ominous orange glow in the distance. It was John's cabin fully ablaze. "No!" Jared coughed. His legs trembling beneath him as he struggled to stand, only to collapse back onto the black sand. His eyes were unable to look away. John's cabin was burning, and the heat of the fire was starting to spread.

Finally able to stand, it was a long search for his truck. Hidden among the dense foliage, in the smoke, he spotted a familiar outline of his vehicle.

Without hesitation, Jared smashed the window with a rock, unlocking the door from the inside. The shattered glass was a clear message that subtlety was no longer an option. Ethan's message was clear: silence Jared at any cost. But Jared was done running.

Sparks under the dash brought his engine roaring to life. He navigated the truck through the shadowy labyrinth of the wood. Each turn, every shadow irritated him, spurred him on.

As he approached Dr. Simonds', the air thickened with soot. The few miles felt like an eternity. The final bend revealed a heart-stopping scene: smoke, thick and acrid, billowed around her home. The sky was deep shades of orange and red. The fire was moving…

BURNING

AS JARED HONKED the horn, thick plumes of smoke threatened Dr. Simonds' home. The warm glow of the porch lights did little to cut through the clouds of thick smoke. Jared passed by a thin road between John's cabin and Dr. Simonds' house—this thin, tenuous line of safety—was all that separated them from the same fate.

As Jared stepped out of his truck, Dr. Simonds emerged from the shadow of her home, her expression a mirror of his own fears. Without needing to speak, they both understood the danger wasn't over. The wind could betray them at any moment, carrying the fire across the road to ignite new horrors.

Jared ran around the side of the house, dragged

the heavy water hose across her lawn, its weight insignificant with him full of adrenaline. He sprayed the perimeter of her property, fighting back against the inferno. Each pass of the water felt like a victory against the danger.

As he worked, sirens called out in the distance, the fire department was containing the blaze. As the embers in the distance settled, Jared put the hose back where he found it. The ash had mixed with the water vapor and covered his body. For all everyone knew, the danger had passed, for now, but the night's events had left its mark.

Jared and Dr. Simonds, exhausted and dirty, sat on her porch. They watched the firefighters extinguish the last of the flames. The night was still warm, the air filled with the smell of char and destruction, but they were safe. For a moment, Jared allowed himself to feel a pang of victory amidst the loss.

Jared breathed in relief, "You're okay." Their eyes met as the distant sound of sirens still echoed in the air.

Dr. Simonds leaned against him, her head resting on his shoulder, a silent gesture of gratitude and comfort. "Thank you," she whispered, her voice hoarse from the smoke. "For everything. Do you know what was burning?" The concern in her eyes reflecting the flaking red lights through the trees.

Dr. Simonds' expression was a mix of relief and horror when she saw Jared's condition—soaked and shivering. She notices his shredded clothes were clinging to his skin. Her hands guided him up the steps, helping him inside, away from the suffocating smoke. Inside he was careful to keep the black goop from her furniture that was clinging to him.

Jared's voice carried the weight of betrayal, making each word heavier than the last. "It's Ethan... Ethan Cross," he confesses, his eyes searching Dr. Simonds' for any sign of recognition or understanding. The words taste of deception and soot. "He's behind the dumping, and now he's trying to cover his tracks." The cold realization of the situation set in on him. "He's after me. I need to call one of my old friends."

"Do you know their number?"

"Yeah," Jared noted, accepting her phone. After a few rings John's voice rang clear in her phone. "This is John, leave me a message."

"Hey, buddy, it's Ethan Cross who's behind all this. Call me back at this number. I lost my phone last night, but they're after me." Hanging up he looked into her eyes. "John knows about Ethan as well. I need to get back to my place in Elmhurst."

Dr. Simonds' phone buzzed. It was a message from John:

> Who's this? I don't have this number in my phone.

> Hey John, it's Jared, I know it's late.

> I need you to give me a call.

I cant,

I'm on the phone with Salvo PD. Apparently my house was on fire. Are you alright?

> Yeah, it was Ethan Cross,

> I'm going to be heading back to Elmhurst as soon as possible.

When can we get together?

> The sooner the better, I can meet you at the pond tomorrow morning.

Jared looked out at the thinning smoke as he handed the phone back to Dr. Simonds, "Thank you for letting me use your phone."

After she read the text she inquired, "Of course. Was the cabin you were staying at John's?"

"Yes," he stated staring out the window at the smoke. "Ethan saw me taking photos of them when they were dumping."

Dr. Simonds saw his condition. Her declaration was firm, her resolve clear as she connected with his eyes. "Well, sticking around here isn't a goal of mine. If you want the paperwork I have, you'll have to take me with you. These documents are my life's work. I'm not about to hand them over and hide," she said, locking eyes with Jared, her stance unwavering. "You want my evidence? I'm coming with you. I'm not going to be a sitting duck here, waiting for whatever comes next."

"By the way, Dr. Simonds, the fish burnt up in the house…"

"Please, call me Jillian," she countered.

The moon hung low in the sky as it broke through the smoke. After a shower, he stepped out to a simple meal she had prepared. They didn't know what was going to happen next, but the night was theirs. The fire was gone. As they talked, laughed, and shared stories of their lives, their problems seemed to fade. It was the first time he had seen this side of her.

Dr. Simonds, usually so composed, let her guard down, her laughter more genuine, her smiles brighter. They found something in each other, their life had been missing. As the night deepened, so did the secrets on their lips. Bonding so that no matter what lay ahead, they would face it together.

At daybreak, before the sun came up, they packed up her car and took one last look at Salvo. There was still a smoky tone in the air. Driving passed John's cabin, nothing could erase the scars of the burn site on the beach. The charred remains of the cabin stood as a stark reminder of what Ethan was willing to do to stop them. Together, they were going to Elmhurst…

RETURNING TO THE ABYSS

IN THE EERIE CALM of the rising sun, Jared and Dr. Simonds made their way back to Elmhurst.

"Do you have a plan?" Dr. Simonds asked, filling the air on the ride home.

"To get to Elmhurst and get a copy of your findings to John," Jared clarified. "I don't want anyone to know what you've got on you. I don't want anything tied back to you at all."

The drive wasn't long but Jared pointed out landmarks of his hometown as they passed by. "And this is it," Jared gestured.

The pond was a stagnant mirror, reflecting the waning light. The soft hues of the sunrise highlighted the oily sheen of pollution that clung to its surface. As they approached, something didn't feel right. As they stepped out, the closer they got, the more wrong it felt. The scene was exactly how he left it. Even the truck waiting to drain the pond hadn't moved. John's truck hadn't moved. Through the oil swirling on the surface, Jared spotted something in the pond. A blurry figure disrupted the stillness, a recognizable shape under the water.

His pulse quickened as he asked for her phone to call John. John's phone rang, the tone carrying an echo across the water, haunting the still air. The vibration caused the hair on the back of their necks to stand up. The phone was here, yet it went unanswered. Concern mounted between each hollow tone.

The surface of the pond rippled, revealing a motionless human form underwater. Panic rose in his throat, a stark contrast to the pond's deceptive calm. "Something's wrong," he whispered to Dr. Simonds, his voice barely hiding his dread. Hanging up the phone Jared knelt at the water's edge, peering into its depths.

Jared called Allen, desperate for reassurance. To gain something in the fleeting moment. Who was he looking at in the water?

Rushing, Jared dialed Allen, "Hey Man, I planned to meet John this morning at the pond. Have you heard from him?" Without missing a beat, Allen's urgent voice cut through, "Get out now! Right now!"

Ethan Cross emerged menacingly from the shadows. The feeble light revealed the evil grin slicing across his face. Ethan sneered, flaunting John's phone in his waving hand. "Expecting someone else? I was wondering who your little friend was," he snarled, glaring at Dr. Simonds.

Jared's jaw tightened. Every breath felt like a countdown, every heartbeat a thunderous drum.

Ethan advanced with predatory grace. A revolver in his other hand caught intermittent glints of light. "Bet you recognize my tanker now, don't you? The one to drain the pond? A real shame. I'm surprised you didn't catch on," he tsked.

The faint smell of chemicals mingled with the rising tension. "How long do you think you've been texting me?" His laugh was cold as he raised his revolver. Not even the shadows could hide the storm that was brewing—a storm Jared could never prepare for…

Thank you for joining us on this journey. As someone living with Parkinson's, each word I've written represents not just an expression of my thoughts, but a defiance against a condition that seeks to limit me. This book is more than a story or a collection of ideas it's a piece of my life, a dialog I cherish with you.

Thank you for joining us on this journey. As someone living with Parkinson's, each word I've written represents not just an expression of my thoughts, but a defiance against a condition that seeks to limit me. This book is more than a story or a collection of ideas; it's a piece of my life, an embodiment of perseverance, and a dialogue I cherish with you.

Your support means the world to me. Knowing that you have spent time in my created world gives me immense joy and motivates me to keep writing, despite the challenges posed by Parkinson's. This condition may try to shake my resolve, but with readers like you, I find the strength to hold steady and continue my passion for writing.

Your support means the world to me. Knowing that you have spent time in my created world gives me immense joy and motivates me to keep writing, despite the challenges posed by Parkinson's. This condition may try to shake my resolve, but with readers like you, I find the strength to hold steady and continue my passion for writing.

Thank you for your encouragement, your empathy, and for being apart of my story. I hope this book touched you in some way and that we can continue this conversation in the pages of my next endeavor

Thank you for your encouragement, your empathy, and for being part of my story. I hope this book has touched you in some way and that we can continue this conversation in the pages of my next endeavor.

~Brenda FireEagle Biddix

THE SILENT STORY

Like its predecessor, this book comes with a gentle reminder. While the narrative weaves fiction, its rooted in truths that are as unsettling as they are real.

Stay vigilant, stay connected, and may the ripples of this tale stir a greater awareness within you. The people we talk to over our phones, could be anyone…

VISIT
RianMileti.com

JOIN THE CONVERSATION

AHOY THERE, FANTASTIC READER OF POND WATER RIPTIDE! Whether you found it utterly unputdownable or it was not your cup of tea, your thoughts matter to us! As the story continues, who's backstory do you want to hear about? What would you like to know? Dive into a conversation with us by dropping a quick review on Amazon and/or Goodreads. And why stop there? Splash the word on TikTok too and there is a good chance we will respond! Make some waves! We are listening carefully and can't wait to soak in your insights. Plus, we adore sharing standout reviews with our awesome social media following.

http://www.RianMileti.com

Made in the USA
Columbia, SC
24 April 2024

34525162R00046